Whinnie the Lovesick Dragon

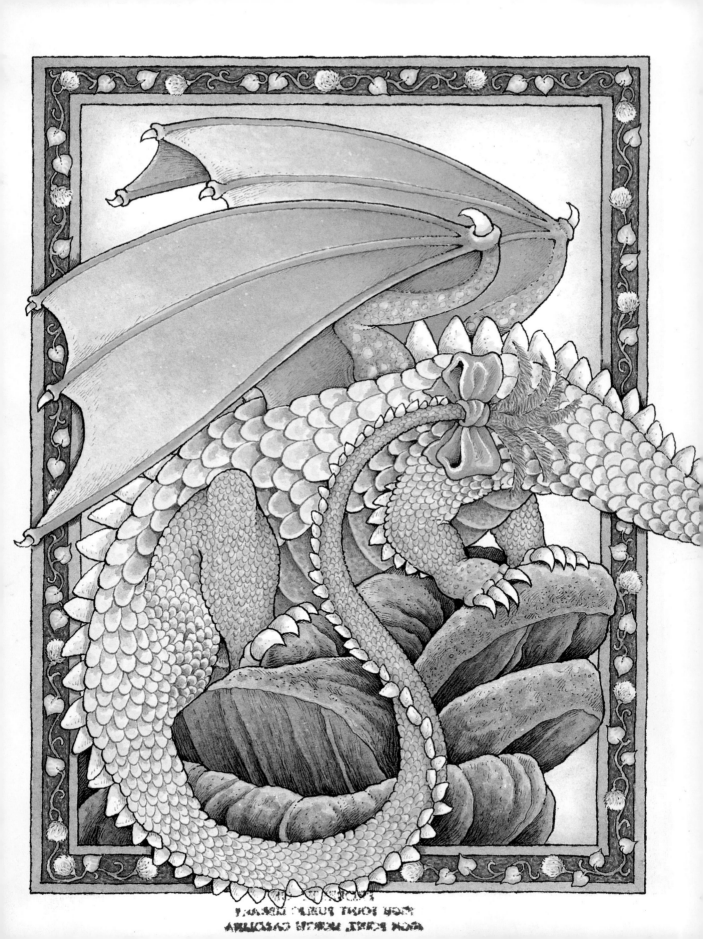

Whinnie
the Lovesick
Dragon

by

Mercer Mayer

illustrations by

Diane Dawson Hearn

Macmillan Publishing Company • New York

Collier Macmillan Publishers • London

Macmillan Publishing Company
866 Third Avenue, New York, N.Y. 10022
Collier Macmillan Canada, Inc.

Printed and bound in Japan
First American Edition
10 9 8 7 6 5 4 3 2 1

The text of this book is set in 16 pt. Sabon.
The illustrations are in pen-and-ink and acrylic wash.

Library of Congress Cataloging-in-Publication Data
Mayer, Mercer, date. 1943-
Whinnie the lovesick dragon.
Summary: Whinnie the dragon falls in love with
Alfred the knight, but she has trouble convincing him to
accept her as a suitable romantic companion.
[1. Dragons—Fiction. 2. Knights and knighthood—
Fiction] I. Hearn, Diane Dawson, ill. II. Title.
PZ7.M462Wi 1986   [E]   85-18886
ISBN 0-02-765180-0

To Jessie,
my daughter
– M.M.

With love to Walter,
my knight in shining armor
– D.D.H.

Whinnie the dragon was in love with Alfred. That would have been fine if Alfred had been a dragon, too. But Alfred was a knight of the king's guards.

Whenever Alfred rode by, Whinnie would look down from her dragon perch and sigh. "Oh, if only he'd notice me!"

But every time Whinnie tried to get Alfred's attention, he ran away. *What's the matter with him?* thought Whinnie. *I'm a luscious-looking dragon. I know what I'll do: I'll trap him and then he'll have to speak to me.*

So Whinnie built her trap. One day, as Alfred rode alone, he spotted a beautiful rose lying on the ground. "Methinks I see a rose lying upon yon heath," he said, in the manner of knights in those days. He dismounted and walked over to the rose. As he bent to pick it up, the ground gave way. *Crash!* Alfred landed in a hole.

"Have no fear, good knight," called a sweet voice from above. "I will rescue you."

"I give thee thanks and will forever be in thy service, fair maid," called Alfred. Down came a rope, and up climbed Alfred. There before him stood Whinnie. "Egad!" cried Alfred. "A dragon has devoured the fair maiden."

"Don't be silly," said Whinnie. "I'm the one who saved you."

"Out of my way, filthy lizard!" cried Alfred crudely.

Her feelings were hurt, but Whinnie was still determined. No matter what he tried, Alfred could not get past her. First she blocked his way with her great tail. Then she blocked his path with her foot, and finally with her whole body. So Alfred took out his sword and gave her a sound whack.

Now everyone knows a knight's sword never could really hurt a dragon, with all its scales and tough skin. But this was the final humiliation. It broke Whinnie's heart that Alfred, the apple of her eye, should smack her. With her eyes full of tears and her head hung low, Whinnie flew away.

To add insult to injury, Alfred shouted after her, "Forsooth, yon dragon flees at just one whack from Alfred the Fearless!" From that time on, Alfred called himself One-Whack Alfred, and he bragged about his great feat wherever he went.

Whinnie flew back to her perch on Dragon Mountain to nurse her broken heart. After a while she thought, *I can't go on like this forever. I must do something to cheer up.* Off she flew to the nearest town for a little shopping, but it didn't help.

Next she went to the theater for a matinee. Of course, as soon as she sat down in the front row, the rest of the audience fled, and Whinnie was alone again with her broken heart.

Maybe a walk in the park will help, she thought. But all
the people ran away, and the park keeper shouted fiercely,
"Dragons are forbidden in the park!" Then he ran, too.

"Perhaps an ocean voyage is the answer," said Whinnie. When she arrived at the dock, everyone fled. When she tried to board the ship, it rolled over with a splash and sank.

Whinnie crawled out of the water and sat on the dock, feeling very low. The commotion had attracted a crowd. They stood back, shouting and throwing tomatoes. With tears in her eyes, Whinnie munched a tomato.

"Call One-Whack Alfred!" someone shouted. "He'll dispatch the dragon!" Soon Alfred appeared. Whinnie's heart skipped a beat, but Alfred stepped up and whacked her again. With one great big sob, Whinnie stretched her wings, rose into the air, and flew away. The crowd cheered and Alfred bowed.

Back home on her perch on Dragon Mountain, Whinnie wiped a tear from her eye and heaved a great big sigh. "Perhaps I'll go visit my friend the wizard. Maybe he can make me feel better."

"What's the matter?" asked the wizard, as Whinnie stuck her sad face through his window.

"Alfred the knight takes no notice of me," answered Whinnie. "Can you help?"

"Well," said the wizard, "sometimes the cure is worse than the problem, but I'll try." The wizard twiddled his beard and paced around the floor. "I know what I can do: I'll turn you into a princess—a most beautiful princess. Your great wings I shall turn into two white horses. Your tail will become a carriage and your scales a fortune in gold bars. Not only will you be beautiful, but you will also be rich."

"I'll try anything," said Whinnie.

The wizard mixed together a concoction of exotic herbs and transformed it into a cherry frappe. Whinnie quickly drank it down through a long straw. Suddenly, her wings fell off and became two prancing horses. Her great tail turned into a beautiful carriage. Her scales fell like rain and became gold bars as they hit the floor. Whinnie shrank smaller and smaller until, standing in the room with the wizard, was a most beautiful princess.

Whinnie thanked the wizard as he helped her into the carriage, loaded with a fortune in gold. Off to town she went.

As Whinnie rode into town, all the people *oohed* and *aahed* to see the beautiful princess in the fine carriage. She went right to the nearest real-estate office and bought the best castle in the land and paid for it with her gold bars. *I'll have a grand ball and invite everyone,* thought Whinnie. She sent out hundreds of invitations, including one to Alfred.

The night of her ball, Whinnie stood by the door and greeted her guests.

The king asked, "Who is this mystery princess?"

All the knights exclaimed, "Isn't she beautiful?"

All the other princesses and fair ladies murmured, "She's much *too* beautiful."

Finally, Alfred arrived. Again, Whinnie's heart skipped a beat. Sure enough, Alfred noticed her and, this time, paid her lots of attention. He even sat next to her at dinner.

But all he talked about was how he could defeat a dragon with one whack of his sword. After dinner they danced, and all Alfred talked about was how beautiful the princess was and how brave he was. As everyone gathered around the fire, Alfred asked the musicians to play a ballad about One-Whack Alfred.

What a terrible bore he is, thought Whinnie.

That evening after the guests had left, Whinnie thought about Alfred. *What he needs is a lesson,* she decided. So she wrote a letter to her Uncle Dragon, who lived high up on Dragon Mountain.

A few days later the townspeople started to talk about the terrible dragon that was roaming the countryside. Again they sent for Alfred to dispatch it. As Alfred marched out with his sword to find the dragon, a great crowd followed him, including Whinnie. They all cheered and urged him on. Soon they came upon the dragon, breathing fire and stamping his feet.

Alfred pulled out his sword, walked up to the dragon, and gave him a whack. The dragon beat his powerful wings and blew Alfred head over heels in the grass. Everyone laughed.

Alfred picked himself up, walked over to the dragon, and gave him another whack. The dragon breathed a giant cloud of fire and smoke down on Alfred. It singed his whiskers and heated his armor so hot that he had to jump into a pond to cool off. The townspeople cried, "What's the matter, Alfred, can't you beat the little old dragon?" Only Whinnie was silent.

Not caring to be laughed at, Alfred walked right up to the
dragon again. This time, before Alfred could give it another
whack, the dragon, with one flip of his tail, sent Alfred clear
across the field. He landed with a splash in the pigpen. Then
Uncle Dragon stretched his mighty wings and flew away to
Dragon Mountain.

All but Whinnie went home shaking their heads and muttering, "Alfred couldn't fight his way out of a watermelon patch."

Whinnie found Alfred lying in the pigpen covered with mud. "Are you hurt?" she asked.

But Alfred didn't answer; he just groaned. Whinnie crawled into the mud and tried to help Alfred to his feet.

"Well, Alfred, have you had enough of being a knight?" a voice said. Whinnie and Alfred looked up to see the wizard.

"What do you mean?" asked Whinnie.

"Well," said the wizard, "Alfred used to be a dragon just like you, Whinnie, but he decided that being a knight would be much better. Right, Alfred?"

"Right," answered Alfred, pouring muddy water out of his helmet.

"When I was a dragon," said Whinnie, "you always whacked me."

"I'm sorry," said Alfred.

"I forgive you," said Whinnie.

To make a long story short, the wizard whipped up another magic cherry frappe and gave one straw to Alfred and the other to Whinnie. In a flash they were both dragons again and feeling much better about it. Whinnie and Alfred flew back to Dragon Mountain and lived happily ever after, of course.

But the wizard is still very busy, for the world is full of people who are really dragons at heart.